kale

sawbuck

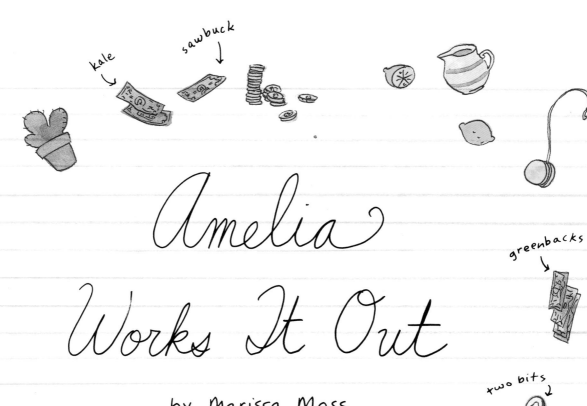

red cent

greenbacks

smacker

Amelia
Works It Out

by Marissa Moss
(and here's-my-card Amelia)

two bits

dough

American Girl™

cash

Arf!

Professional Journal
Writer

Have pencil, will travel.

Amelia

moolah

bucks

← walking the dog

This notebook is dedicated
to Kathleen,
a very hard worker.

really walking
the dog ↑

But remember
what your mother
told you— if
you can't say
something
nice, don't say
anything at all!

Pleasant Company
Publications
8400 Fairway Place
Middleton, Wisconsin
53562

Yip!

Book Design by Amelia

Library of Congress Cataloging-in-Publication Data
Moss, Marissa
Amelia works it out / by Marissa Moss
p.   cm. "American girl." "An Amelia book."
Summary: Amelia draws on her artistic talent to earn money
for something special that she really wants.

ISBN 1-58485-081-7 (hc)   ISBN 1-58485-080-9 (pb)
[1. Moneymaking projects-Fiction. 2. Artists-Fiction.]

I. Title.
PZ7.M8535 Aj 2000   99-089850
[Fic]--dc21

First Pleasant Company Publications printing, 2000

how much money I made!
↙

Manufactured in Singapore
00 01 02 03 04 05 06 TWP 10 9 8 7 6 5 4 3 2 1

↑
how much money I owe

Yawn!

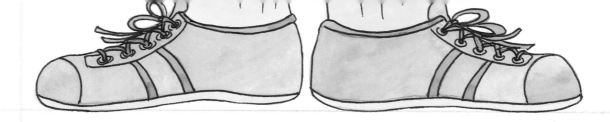

These are my feet now, in regular, plain old shoes — but I'm working on changing that. I never used to think about my feet, as long as they were comfortable, but that was before LIGHTSCAPE/NIGHTSCAPE shoes were invented. Now everybody at school has them. Except me. And they're really cool!

me, in my boring shoes

my best friend, Carly, in cool new LIGHTSCAPE/NIGHTSCAPE shoes

dull, listless look — no pep here

limp hair, saddened by the thought of lumpy shoes

slouching posture — body is too disappointed with lousy footwear to stand up straight

bright, sunshiny smile to go with sunshiny shoes

happy, bouncy body perked up by snazzy footsies

feet feel so light they practically fly!

feet practically drag themselves around in these blecchy shoes

Here's why LIGHTSCAPE/NIGHTSCAPE shoes are <u>so</u> neat-o!

They have a picture printed on them that's sensitive to light.

In the dark or low light, you see a night scene.

In strong light, it becomes a day scene.

There are all kinds of choices of pictures on the shoes.

a jungle

eek! eyes!

an ocean

glow-in-the-dark fish

too hot for animals in the day

cool eno[ugh] to come out [at] nigh[t]

a desert (not a dessert)

It's hard to decide which one's best.

This is dessert.

I mean, shoes like that are as close to magic as you can possibly get. I BEGGED Mom to get me a pair, but she said they're too expensive and that my old shoes are fine anyway.

I showed her how scuffed up my old shoes were, but she wasn't convinced.

I tried the angel act (after all, it worked when I wanted to go to Space Camp).

All that begging made Mom mad. She sent me to my room and told me to think of all the times I really wanted something but didn't like it after I actually got it. So here's my list of stuff that seems good at first but, when you think about it, isn't that great after all.

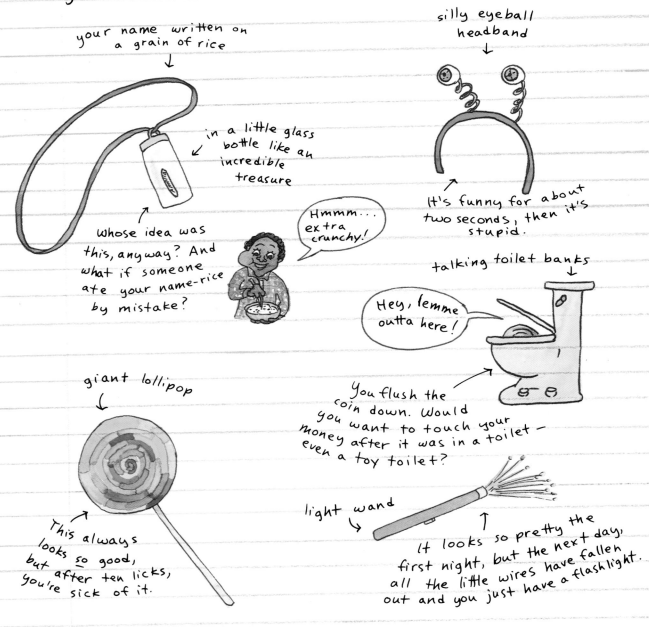

your name written on a grain of rice

in a little glass bottle like an incredible treasure

Whose idea was this, anyway? And what if someone ate your name-rice by mistake?

Hmmm... extra crunchy!

silly eyeball headband

It's funny for about two seconds, then it's stupid.

talking toilet banks

Hey, lemme outta here!

You flush the coin down. Would you want to touch your money after it was in a toilet — even a toy toilet?

giant lollipop

This always looks so good, but after ten licks, you're sick of it.

light wand

It looks so pretty the first night, but the next day, all the little wires have fallen out and you just have a flashlight.

Even Carly tried to talk me out of wanting the shoes. Easy for _her_ to say — she has some already!

My mom wouldn't buy them for me, either. My grandma did. But I didn't really care if I got them or not. It was _her_ idea.

That was bad enough. Then the **WORST** happened. My own jelly-roll-nose sister got them. She bought them herself with money she earned babysitting.

Oh, Ameeeeeelia! I've got something to shoooooooow you!

Even **LIGHTSCAPE/NIGHTSCAPE** shoes can't transform _her_ smelly old feet! I feel sorry for the shoes.

She picked the cityscape. That's the kind _I_ want!

That does it! If Cleo can make enough money to buy them, so can I. Except I'm too young to babysit, so I'll have to think of something else. It's not fair that she gets paid to watch kids when I'd be much better at it. Why do people judge you by how old you are?

Cleo gets _every_thing before I do — the clothes I wear, the bike I ride. If the only way I get **LIGHTSCAPE/NIGHTSCAPE** shoes is as a hand-me-down, I'll scream!

Things Cleo got to do before me:

lose a tooth

ride a bike

get an allowance

go on a roller coaster

spend a week at a sleep-away camp

wear practically all my clothes — at least Mom doesn't believe in hand-me-down underwear (socks are bad enough)

← earn money →

Since Mom won't buy me my shoes, I'll have to buy them myself. What can I do to make money (preferably something Cleo hasn't

Cleo said she'd pay me to clean her room — a whole 25¢. You'd have to pay me a LOT more than that to touch her gross, germy things. But she gave me a good idea for _another_ way to earn money. I made a business card and slipped it under her door.

<u>Guarantee</u>   <u>Your</u>   <u>Privacy</u> !

Tired of being eavesdropped on when you have friends over? Worried your mom will hear about all the bad things you did? Then this is the PROTECTION you need! Pay Amelia the measly sum of $5 (that's right, folks, a <u>mere</u> $5!) and she will leave you utterly and completely ALONE!

No more ears under the door!

No more eyes peeping through the keyhole!

Unfortunately, Cleo didn't respond to my generous offer the way I thought she would. Instead she came storming out of her room and threatened to flatten me if I ever came near her door when she had friends over.

Cleo snorting with fury →

You little brat! I'll pay you good if I catch you spying on me!

← A knuckle sandwich isn't the payment I want.

So I need to think of another way to earn money. Anyway, I only have <u>one</u> sister. I need a job where I can get <u>lots</u> of customers.

I wrote to Nadia, my old best friend. (She's still my faraway best friend and Carly's my close-by best friend. Nadia always has good ideas.) →

· FASHIONS OF THE SIXTIES ·

Dear Nadia,
   You know I don't usually follow fads, but I <u>really</u> want a pair of LIGHTSCAPE/NIGHTSCAPE shoes. <u>Not</u> because everyone else is wearing them, but because I think they're so cool.
   I'm trying to figure out how to make money so I can buy them. It's not easy! Any suggestions?
      luv, Amelia
   yours till the shoe buckles!

F A D S 20
BELL BOTTOMS

Nadia Kurz
61 South St.
Barton, CA
91010

Carly gets paid to do extra chores, like washing windows or mowing the lawn, but <u>my</u> mom pays so little for that kind of thing, it would take FOREVER for me to earn enough.

me, old and gray by the time → I get my LIGHTSCAPE/NIGHTSCAPE shoes

still stooped over, even with cool shoes ↓

Yee-haw! I finally got those shoes I've wanted for ages!

old-people size - do your feet shrink and wrinkle up the way your face does? →

lemon + water + sugar = dough!

In the movies, when kids want to make money, they set up a lemonade stand. It was worth a try. Carly helped me juice the lemons. We added lots of sugar. Then, to make our lemonade special, I put in a few drops of blue food coloring. Carly **wanted** red, so she added some, and we ended up with purple lemonade. It looked <u>so</u> cool! We got out some paper cups and made a sign, and we were open for business.

potential customers
↓

Purple lemonade? Blecch!

Don't kids know that lemonade is supposed to be yellow — or pink?

You would think there would be crowds of people eager for a glass of our delicious purple lemonade. You would think there would be a line around the block. You would think we would sell at least 🔲 cup. We didn't. Not one!

unfortunately, we drank all the lemonade we had left — definitely a BIG mistake!

lemon pucker →

way too full and sloshy →

FRESH COLD LEMONADE

25¢ a cup
COME AND GET IT!

lemonade bloat — my pants were ready to explode!

Business Lesson #1: It doesn't matter how great <u>you</u> think the stuff you're selling is. If people don't want to buy it, you won't make money. It's like one of Ms. Busby's word problems in math class: if you make 25 glasses of lemonade at 25¢ a glass, but don't sell any, how much money do you make?

Zero! Nada! The Big Empty! Zip! Goose Egg! ⊙!
It all equals NOTHING!

At least I got a postcard from Nadia — <u>that's</u> something

Dear Amelia,
 ~~Those shoes~~ must be
everywhere! I admit
they're cool, but I hate
to be like everyone else.
I wouldn't want people
to think I wore them
just to be one of the crowd.
And you know how my dad
feels about fads — no way he'd
get me a pair. Somehow I can't
spend my own money on clothes.

FADS
PLATFORM
20 HEELS 20

Amelia
564 North Homecrest
Oopa, Oregon
97881

luv, Nadia
yours till the
shoe polishes!

    So I'm not the only person in the universe who doesn't
have those shoes — Nadia doesn't either! That make
me feel a little better, but she's too far away for it
to make a BIG difference.

    Nadia didn't offer any job suggestions, but she
probably thinks I shouldn't waste my money on shoe
since she wouldn't. I don't want to spend mone
on clothes, either, but LIGHTSCAPE/NIGHTSCAPE
shoes aren't just footwear —
they're magic!

They seem so fun — like they could turn you into a happier, lighter, bouncier person. On TV, people fly in their amazing, beautiful shoes. I mean, I don't believe the commercials. I know shoes can't make you fly. But still, they do <u>something</u> to you. (Unless you're Cleo — then you're beyond LIGHTSCAPE/NIGHTSCAPE magic.)

I could PRETEND I'm flying in those shoes.

I tore this ad out of a magazine. I hope it's not the closest I get to owning a pair of LIGHTSCAPE/NIGHTSCAPE shoes.

LIGHT UP YOUR WORLD WITH LIGHTSCAPE/NIGHTSCAPE ™ SHOES!

Drinking a certain soda doesn't automatically make you cool. (But it will make you burp!)

No matter what kind of shampoo you use, your hair will NOT bounce. (And why should you want it to bounce anyway? It's hair, not a ball!

It may look delicious on TV, but you can never make it taste that way at home.

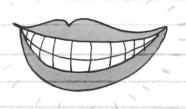

I don't care how many mints you eat or how much gum you chew — if you want fresh breath, you still have to BRUSH YOUR TEETH!

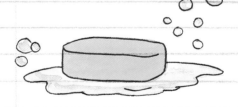

Soap is soap is soap is soap is soap is soap is soap. It doesn't matter which brand you use — it's still soap!

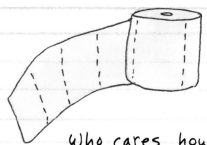

Who cares how soft toilet paper is? You're not sleeping on it!

TO BELIEVE COMMERCIALS

Driving that new car will not make you rich, beautiful, and popular — but you won't have to take the bus.

All chocolates will melt in your hand.

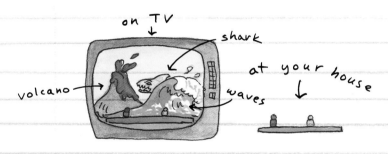

The game on TV looks really cool because they add all this stuff around it that's not part of the game you get in the box.

It's not zany fun — it's just breakfast cereal.

Nothing you eat will really turn you into a superhero.

Fast-food joints don't mean it when they say they'll make food any way you want.

Maybe Nadia's right — I should just forget about LIGHTSCAPE/NIGHTSCAPE shoes.

At home I hear Nadia's voice inside my head.

Remember, it's not what you wear but who you are that matters.

But at school I hear other voices.

Here's how I yo-yo:

Don't you wanna be cool, like me?

Are you in or out?

What kind of person wears shoes like those?

① Leave yo-yo on table. Look! It's taking a nap!

At recess today I got an idea for a job that just might work. Carly, Maya, and I were jumping double Dutch, and so were a lot of other kids. But I noticed that most kids weren't jumping rope — they were playing with yo-yos. Personally, I'm not a great yo-yoer, but I _am_ good at fixing them. And yo-yos need fixing if they're played with a lot.

yo-yo troubles

detached string

twisted-up string

gunk in between sides

② Swing yo-yo back and forth before someone's eyes — AMAZING yo-yo hypnotism!

So I decided to do yo-yo repair! Since I can't advertise on TV, I made business cards to pass out to possible customers.

③ Roll yo-yo along the floor while saying "Toooot toooot" — it's doing the choo-choo train!

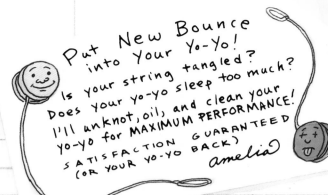

Put New Bounce into Your Yo-Yo!

Is your string tangled? Does your yo-yo sleep too much? I'll unknot, oil, and clean your yo-yo for MAXIMUM PERFORMANCE!

SATISFACTION GUARANTEED (OR YOUR YO-YO BACK) *amelia*

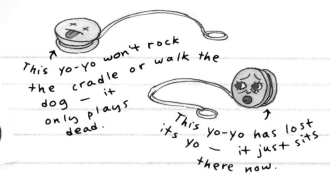

This yo-yo won't rock the cradle or walk the dog — it only plays dead.

This yo-yo has lost its yo — it just sits there now.

← I gave out business cards like this one.

Making my business cards made me think about what the perfect job would be. I mean, there are some jobs that are so GREAT, I'd do them for <u>nothing</u>!

DREAM JOBS

COMIC BOOK EDITOR

Very exciting! You forgot a period here, but that's it.

MATTRESS TESTER

Let's see, pretty cozy — not too hard, not too soft, it's just... zzzzz...

They're tough but someone's got to do them.

ICE CREAM TASTER
~ yum, yum ~

Hmm, needs a touch more chocolate.

MOVIE REVIEWER

I give it a big thumbs-up! Good popcorn, too!

CHILDREN'S BOOK AUTHOR and ILLUSTRATOR

I get to write and draw all day!

It looks like fun — and it is!

HOLIDAY WINDOW PAINTER

Then there are jobs I'd NEVER want to do, no matter what you paid me!

yo-yo repair tools

 oil

 replacement strings

 soft cloth for polishing — really an old T-shirt

Fixing yo-yos may not be a DREAM job, but it's a job. I'm actually getting customers — LOTS of them! I couldn't charge a lot, though, or no one would hire me. So even though 9 kids asked me to fix their yo-yos, I earned a grand total of $13 (and one kid paid me with a comic book).

If this was a math problem, it'd go like this: Lulu earns 50¢ an hour mowing lawns. If she wants to save $50, how many hours will she have to work? Will she have time to do anything else

poor, exhausted Lulu — worn out for a mere $6

Business Lesson #2: If you have a service people want, but they won't pay a lot of money for, you won't make enough money for it to be worth your time.

I want time to equal lots of money — not pennies.

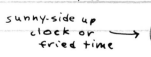 sunny-side up clock or fried time

 =

 or =

 ?

I've got to figure out something I can do that people want and that will pay me what I want.

 The comic book I got for cleaning Max's yo-yo was a good one, but it didn't get me any closer to buying my shoes.

Carly and I were walking home from school when I got an idea for a GREAT job.

YIP!

BEWARE OF DOG

We always pass this house with a little dog right next door to a house with a HUGE dog.

That gave me the idea — I could walk people's dogs! I like animals, I can walk, I'm not too young to hold a leash, lots of people have dogs but don't have time to walk them, and grown-ups will pay more than kids do — it's PERFECT!

I made business cards to advertise my new service. I'm calling it WOOF WALKERS. Carly helped me put my cards up all over the place — the library, grocery stores, post office, pet food store, anywhere dog owners might go.

WOOF WALKERS
No dog too big, no walk too long, no bark too loud.
Call Amelia, master dog-walker.

WOOF WALKERS
No dog too big, no walk too long, no bark too loud.
Call Amelia, master dog-walker.

since I put up my cards, I've been noticing dogs EVERYWHERE. I wonder which ones I'll get.

bald dog with giant ears →

little dust-mop dog →

squashed-face dog →

Carly thinks my cards are really cute. She asked if I would make her a business card. She doesn't have a job yet, but someday she wants to be an investigative reporter.

I asked her to tell me about reporting so I'd know what to put on the card. →

It's important to ask the five W's — who, what, when, where, why. And don't forget the one with a W at the end — How.

She's been a good friend to help me in my job searching. →

← Carly's notebook She's always prepared to write something down.

Here are my five W's:
Why does Cleo get everything cool first? What can I do to earn money? Who will be my customers? Where will I find a job? When will I have my own LIGHTSCAPE/NIGHTSCAPE shoes? And how will it feel to finally wear them? I can't wait to answer that last question!

The business card I made for Carly looked like this. She loved it!

↓

•THE FIVE W's:
ho
hat
hen
here
hy
Carly Darrow
INVESTIGATIVE REPORTER
no stone. left unturned
always gets the scoop.

But if anyone has noticed my dog-walking cards, I sure can't tell. No one's called to hire me yet. I'm waaaaiting!

My poor piggy bank is starving!

side view of hollow piggy

↑ front view of hungry, caved-in piggy

I wish I didn't want those shoes so much. Getting work is just as hard as doing work.

It's so unfair that Cleo can earn money babysitting when all she probably does is eat popcorn and watch TV. I'm willing to really work, but no one will give me a chance. I'm not even asking to take care of kids — just dogs!

BURP!

Cleo's overfed piggy bank (really a hoggy bank!)

Cleo's idea of babysitting is sitting and stuffing her face.

Will you play Candy Land with me?

Go watch a video — I'm busy!

Tonight was the worst. She got home from her job chomping on leftover chow mein, and waved all this money in my face.

Mom says Cleo should save her money, but does she? No!!

Hmmm... What should I buy next?

Let's count now...

Doggy business — what dogs do on walks: →

mmm!

smell EVERYTHING!

Ah, aged sandwich crusts!

↑ eat gross things they find on the ground

Just as she was gloating, the phone rang and it was for me. I FINALLY GOT MY FIRST JOB!! **WOOF WALKERS** is in business! Mr. Singh wants me to walk Precious, his basset hound. He sprained his ankle (Mr. Singh, not Precious), so he can't do it for the next week or two. That means I have a job for 2 weeks, and he'll pay me $5 a day.

Another math problem:
2 weeks = 14 days, 14 days at $5 a day = $70! I'll be rich, rich, RICH!

Today was my first day at work. Maybe a long time ago Precious was precious, but now she's old and smelly. She's almost too old to walk. I feel like I'm dragging her down the sidewalk.

Arf, ARF, ARF!

↑ bark at anything that moves

C'mon, Precious. Don't you want a walky-poo?

← legs aren't moving at all

When I got home from pulling Precious, there was a message for me — __another__ job! A guy down the street wants me to walk his terrier for a few days. Maybe the terrier will perk up Precious. It'll probably be easier to walk two dogs at once than drag one old dog like Precious.

The terrier's name is Yipster because she yips all the time. At least she's not old — she's definitely got pep!

I thought Yipster would make walking Precious easier, but it hasn't turned out that way at all. Precious still doesn't want to go anywhere, but now I have Yipster pulling me while I pull Precious. It would be funny in a cartoon, but it's not in real life.

arf arf arf arf arf arf arf arf arf arf arf arf

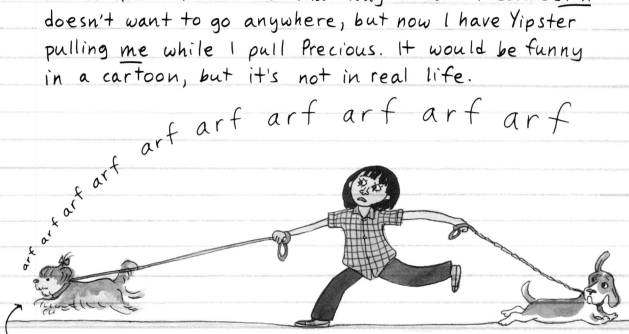

Also, Yipster chases cats, squirrels, and little kids, so I have to pull her away from something all the time. I'm getting very strong arms.

Just when I was getting the hang of walking two dogs at once, I got another call. Ms. Friese from across the street asked me to walk her Irish setter this week because she has to work late. I didn't want to say no, because it means more money, but now I have three dogs to walk. Well, I guess since I can handle two, one more won't make a difference.

more math:
$70 (Precious) + $25 (Yipster) + $35 (the Irish setter) = $130!! I've never had that much money. I can buy my shoes and have lots of money left over!

By the time I got to Ms. Friese's house, I'd already imagined earning so much money, I didn't know what to do with it. I almost forgot that I had work to do first. Rusty reminded me right away.

Irish setters are BIG dogs.

Rusty was so excited to see me, he drooled all over my feet (good thing I was wearing regular old shoes).

Uh, down, boy, down!

I'm a small person.

With Rusty, Yipster, and Precious, I wasn't sure which dog to follow and which dog to pull in. Rusty decided for me — he was definitely going to lead. He ran so fast Yipster couldn't even yip. She had to save all her breath for keeping up with him. Precious, of course, didn't even try, but she weighed him down as much as she could. And me, I was somewhere in the middle, holding on to all their leashes so hard I got rope burns.

I was getting pretty tired of being walked (really "run") by Rusty instead of me walking him. Today when I walked the dogs, I decided things would be different. I didn't let Rusty yank me around — I started out with his leash really short and tight. We were walking, not running, very nicely (even Precious actually moved her legs once in a while) when

DISASTER STRUCK!!

Yipster saw a squirrel and, of course, started yapping and running after it. That got Rusty all excited. Then when he saw the squirrel, he really went wild! Rusty took off chasing it and, when it ran up a tree in someone's yard, he followed it. Rusty jumped over the fence into the yard, pulling all of us along. Yipster ran through the fence slats, Precious was dragged up against the fence, and I was left on the other side with her, yelling at the dogs to stop. They didn't stop. They barked like maniacs, plowing through the flower beds, racing around the tree. I thought things couldn't get worse — but they did!

That's when the lightbulb went on! The best part of all my jobs was drawing business cards for them. If I make cards — <u>greeting</u> cards — for other people, I can get paid for what I have fun doing! I was so excited, I gave Cleo a big hug and kiss.

Thank you, thank you, thank you!

Geeez, I just wanted one little card.

Carly thinks my card idea is terrific. After school she went with me to the art store to get supplies. I used my yo-yo and **WOOF WALKERS** money to buy paper and envelopes.

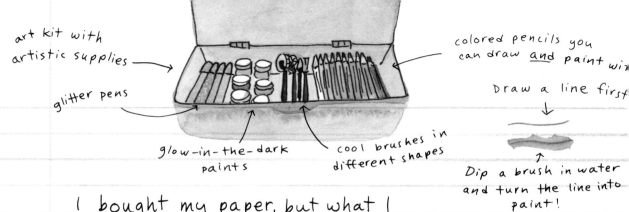

art kit with artistic supplies →

glitter pens

colored pencils you can draw *and* paint wi...

Draw a line first
↓

glow-in-the-dark paints

cool brushes in different shapes

Dip a brush in water and turn the line into paint!

   I bought my paper, but what I really wanted was this cool art kit. Too bad I didn't have enough money for it. (That's the story of my life — I never have enough money for ANYTHING important — at least, not yet!)

   With my new supplies I made cards, stationery, and postcards. I used my old pencils, markers, and paints. It was a lot of fun, and I love the idea that people might think my drawings are good enough to actually pay money for them!

   Maybe next I can draw comic books, make copies at the copy store, and sell Amelia comics.

handmade postcards — I sent one to Nadia and one to my Japanese pen ...

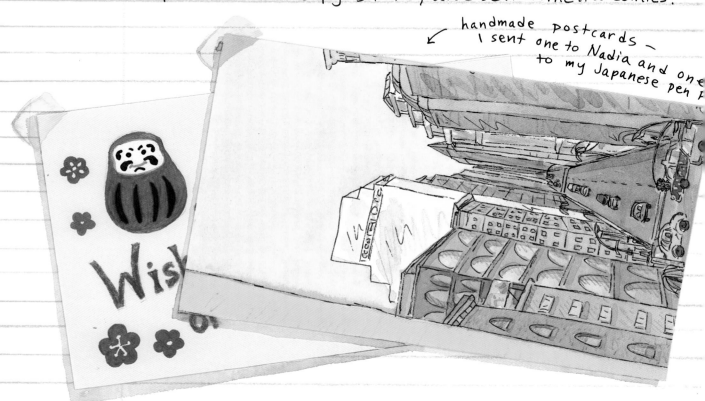

Wish...

Amelia's Art Cards

An elephant never forgets, it's your birthday!

Happy Birthday cards

Wow! You've grown. It must be your birthday!

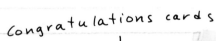

congratulations cards

YOU DID IT!
fill in the blank

HOORAY FOR YOU!

Thank-you cards

You shouldn't have — but, I'm glad you did!

Oooh! I love it!

I'm flying to tell you...

small so you don't have to write a lot

Since making cards was Cleo's idea, I gave her first pick. She chose a giraffe card for Gigi. I brought the rest with me to school.

I was showing them to Carly when Charisse came over and asked to see them. I always thought Charisse was perfect, but she says she's <u>not</u> a perfect drawer. She loved the bear card, so she bought it. My first sale! (Aside from family, which doesn't count).

Charisse showed my card to her friends, so at recess th<u>ey</u> wanted to get cards, too.

Look at mine!

Look at <u>mine</u>!

By lunchtime, a <u>lot</u> of kids knew about my cards. Leah, who's a good artist herself, bought one.

Susie bought one, and so did Angela

I love it!

Even one of the hairnet ladies wanted a birthday card.

Max chose one.

Thanks!

Tasty drawing, hon!

After that, everywhere I went, <u>someone</u> asked for a card!

Luckily I had one left for Mom to buy.

It's great, honey!

Hilary, who used to be so mean to me, paid me $1 for a thank-you card.

My teacher, Ms. Busby, bought ⸜2⸝ postcards!

I DID IT!

I finally, _finally_, FINALLY earned enough money to buy my own LIGHTSCAPE/NIGHTSCAPE shoes! Carly and I are going to walk to the shoe store after school tomorrow so I can get them.

wallet bulging with hard-earned money

Even with my ordinary shoes, I feel like I'm walking on air!

I tried on a pair and they fit! I have to admit, my feet looked GREAT in those shoes. I really wanted them, really I did... at least I thou<u>gh</u>t I did. But somehow when it was my turn in line and the cashier was ready to ring them up, I just couldn't buy them. I mean, I worked <u>so</u> hard for that money, I wanted to buy something really special with it. I thought that the **LIGHTSCAPE/NIGHTSCAPE** shoes were that special thing, but they weren't. Maybe all along I <u>had</u> wanted them just because everyone else had them.

Carly couldn't believe it. →

After all that, you're <u>not</u> getting them?

After all that, I don't really <u>want</u> them.

Mom was right. Sometimes when you get something you've really wanted, you wonder why you ever wanted it in the first place.

And it's different when you have to buy it yourself instead of getting it as a present.

It's hard to break your piggy

But I <u>did</u> want something, and this time I was sure what that something was.

"C'mon," I told Carly. "Let's get what I've been saving for."

"I thought the shoes were what you were saving for," Carly said.

"Nope," I said. Carly looked at me like I was crazy, but she followed me down the block. We went into the right store this time, and I couldn't stop smiling when I paid for my brand-new, neato-mosquito

Carly smiled, too. ↓

Now that's smart! With the art kit, you can make more cards and earn more money.

I've got ideas for lots more cards!
↓

It's that time again!

↑
Birthday reminder cards, so people don't forget to send you presents.

I **LOVE** my art kit, and I've already made my first card with it. I gave it to Cleo. After all, she _was_ my first customer — one thing I didn't mind her being first at — and she gave me the idea.

It looked like this. ↓

To my number sister!

Look, Ma, no hands!

congrats! your braces are off!

↑
Special occasions that people need to notice.
↓

YEAH! Your ears are pierced

Business Lesson #4: Find what you love to do, and get paid to do it!

I'll make up my own holidays.
↓

National Cookie Baking Day! Take a bite!

Or, to put it in a math problem:

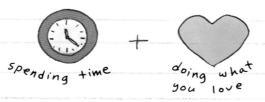

spending time + doing what you love = makes you happy and your piggy bank fat!

That's the kind of math I love!

USEFUL INFORMATION

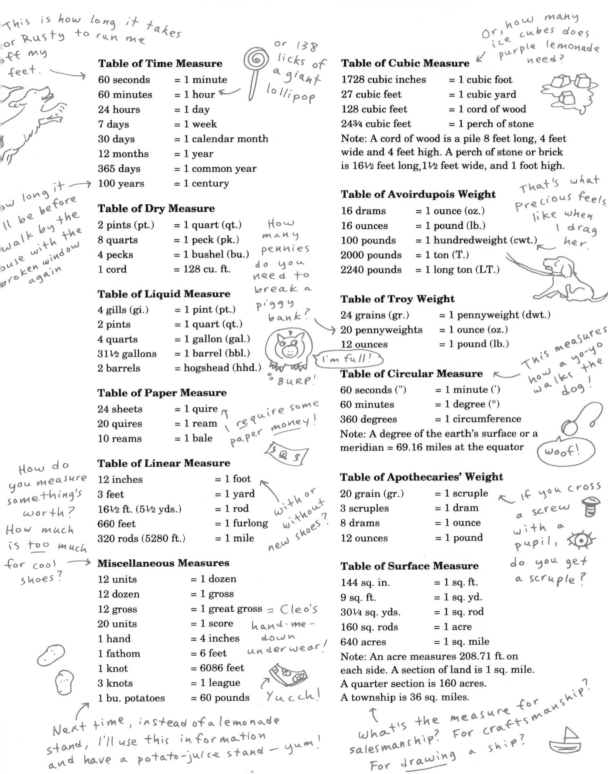

This is how long it takes for Rusty to run me off my feet.

or 138 licks of a giant lollipop

Or, how many ice cubes does purple lemonade need?

Table of Time Measure

60 seconds	= 1 minute
60 minutes	= 1 hour
24 hours	= 1 day
7 days	= 1 week
30 days	= 1 calendar month
12 months	= 1 year
365 days	= 1 common year
100 years	= 1 century

How long it'll be before I walk by the house with the broken window again

Table of Dry Measure

2 pints (pt.)	= 1 quart (qt.)
8 quarts	= 1 peck (pk.)
4 pecks	= 1 bushel (bu.)
1 cord	= 128 cu. ft.

How many pennies do you need to break a piggy bank?

Table of Liquid Measure

4 gills (gi.)	= 1 pint (pt.)
2 pints	= 1 quart (qt.)
4 quarts	= 1 gallon (gal.)
31½ gallons	= 1 barrel (bbl.)
2 barrels	= hogshead (hhd.)

I'm full!

° BURP!

Table of Paper Measure

24 sheets	= 1 quire
20 quires	= 1 ream
10 reams	= 1 bale

I require some paper money!

Table of Linear Measure

12 inches	= 1 foot
3 feet	= 1 yard
16½ ft. (5½ yds.)	= 1 rod
660 feet	= 1 furlong
320 rods (5280 ft.)	= 1 mile

with or without new shoes?

How do you measure something's worth? How much is too much for cool shoes?

Miscellaneous Measures

12 units	= 1 dozen
12 dozen	= 1 gross
12 gross	= 1 great gross
20 units	= 1 score
1 hand	= 4 inches
1 fathom	= 6 feet
1 knot	= 6086 feet
3 knots	= 1 league
1 bu. potatoes	= 60 pounds

= Cleo's hand-me-down underwear!

Yucch!

Next time, instead of a lemonade stand, I'll use this information and have a potato-juice stand — yum!

Table of Cubic Measure

1728 cubic inches	= 1 cubic foot
27 cubic feet	= 1 cubic yard
128 cubic feet	= 1 cord of wood
24¾ cubic feet	= 1 perch of stone

Note: A cord of wood is a pile 8 feet long, 4 feet wide and 4 feet high. A perch of stone or brick is 16½ feet long, 1½ feet wide, and 1 foot high.

Table of Avoirdupois Weight

16 drams	= 1 ounce (oz.)
16 ounces	= 1 pound (lb.)
100 pounds	= 1 hundredweight (cwt.)
2000 pounds	= 1 ton (T.)
2240 pounds	= 1 long ton (LT.)

That's what Precious feels like when I drag her.

Table of Troy Weight

24 grains (gr.)	= 1 pennyweight (dwt.)
20 pennyweights	= 1 ounce (oz.)
12 ounces	= 1 pound (lb.)

This measures how a yo-yo walks the dog!

Table of Circular Measure

60 seconds (")	= 1 minute (')
60 minutes	= 1 degree (°)
360 degrees	= 1 circumference

Note: A degree of the earth's surface or a meridian = 69.16 miles at the equator

woof!

Table of Apothecaries' Weight

20 grain (gr.)	= 1 scruple
3 scruples	= 1 dram
8 drams	= 1 ounce
12 ounces	= 1 pound

If you cross a screw with a pupil, do you get a scruple?

Table of Surface Measure

144 sq. in.	= 1 sq. ft.
9 sq. ft.	= 1 sq. yd.
30¼ sq. yds.	= 1 sq. rod
160 sq. rods	= 1 acre
640 acres	= 1 sq. mile

Note: An acre measures 208.71 ft. on each side. A section of land is 1 sq. mile. A quarter section is 160 acres. A township is 36 sq. miles.

What's the measure for salesmanship? For craftsmanship? For drawing a ship?

Here's what kids have to say about Amelia's
other books and stories . . .

"I'm glad you thought to make <u>My Notebook (with help from Amelia)</u>.
It's a book I can use as my own. It has helped me get started writing my
own notebook. Maybe I could learn to be an author like you one day!"
—Danielle Riep

"I read your stories in <u>American Girl</u> magazine. My favorite character
is Amelia, because she's always writing and thinking up new ideas."
—Shayna McDonald

Sure you can! Read
Amelia's Easy-as-Pie
Drawing Guide!

"Your book was so cool! I couldn't draw
like you for a million bazillion years." ←
—Ariel Cohen

"I love the Amelia books. But where is Amelia's dad?
Read <u>Amelia's</u>   Are the parents divorced? Please tell me."
<u>Family Ties</u> → —Heather Brown
for the answers!

"I wish I had a best friend just like Amelia. You make these notebooks
seem real. The best thing is that they are very funny, and Amelia is just
like a real girl. We share all the same interests!"
—Kristen Ledlow

Manufactured
in Singapore
ISBN 1-58485-080-9

American Girl™

Ages 8 and up
LFP $5.95

9 781584 850809

7 23232 05080 2

WAKE UP AND
SMELL THE COFFEE.

16¢

30¢

SWEETIE-PIE

FIDO

3U-DPG-222